Trouble
on the Track

First published in Great Britain in 2018 by
Piccadilly Press
80-81 Wimpole Street, London, W1G 9RE
www.piccadillypress.co.uk

A CIP catalogue record for this book is available from the British Library.

ISBN: 978–1–848–12635–0
also available as an ebook

1 3 5 7 9 10 8 6 4 2

FLYING FERGUS

Trouble on the Track

CHRIS HOY
with Joanna Nadin

Illustrations by Clare Elsom

Piccadilly
PRESS

Meet Fergus
and his friends...

Fergus

Chimp

Grandpa Herc

Daisy

Jambo Patterson

Mum

Mikey McLeod

Minnie McLeod

Wesley Wallace

Dermot Eggs

Calamity Coogan

Sorcha

Charlie Campbell

Choppy Wallace

Belinda Bruce

. . .and see where they live

Fergus's house

Daisy's house

NAPIER STREET

Herc's Hand-Me-Downs

Bandstand

Play park

CARNOUSTIE COMMON

Bruce's Biscuits

Meet Princess Lily

and her friends. . .

Hector Hamilton

Princess Lily

Unlucky Luke

Percy the Pretty Useless

Demelza

Douglas

Dimmock

Prince Waldorf

Queen Woebegot

King Woebegot

Duke Dastardly

Prince Derek

Knights of No Nonsense

Scary Mary

Team Spirit

Fergus Hamilton was an ordinary nine-year-old boy. He liked baths (but mainly the mud kind), books (but mainly ones with Captain Gadget in), and broad beans (as long as they came with enough ketchup). He didn't like getting up in the mornings (unless it was to ride his bike), going for long walks (unless it was with his dog, Chimp), or any kind of test (unless it was in sports, because he always aced those).

Yes, he was ordinary in almost every way, except one. Because, for a small boy, Fergus Hamilton had an extraordinarily big imagination.

Some days he imagined he was wearing the number one jersey for the Olympic cycling team, just like his hero Spokes Sullivan when he'd won gold two years ago.

Some days he imagined he was wearing the coach's cap for the Palace Pedallers, the cycling team he and his dad had set up in Nevermore (the parallel universe where his dad had been trapped since before Fergus had even been born).

And some days he just imagined he was wearing brand new cycling shoes, the kind that clicked into your pedals and clacked on the ground when you walked. The kind that his mum could definitely never afford.

But this morning Fergus was imagining he was very definitely *not* in Bridie's Brides on Princess Street wearing a tight, itchy suit and green silk tie, with a matching green handkerchief poking out of his top pocket. "Do I really have to?" he asked, as Mum adjusted his collar for what felt like the fiftieth time.

"Och, don't be daft," she replied, still fiddling. "What else are you going to wear to the wedding? Your team strip?"

"Ooh, can we?" yelped Fergus's best friend Daisy, as she fidgeted in her puffy green dress. "I look like a lampshade in this!"

"Herc?" Mum turned to Grandpa, who was trying to admire himself in the mirror.

Grandpa grimaced. "I'm with the kids," he said. "I feel like a proper penguin in this get-up. And what about the expense?"

"Honestly!" Mum exclaimed. "This is the most important day for me since . . . well, since our Fergie here was born, and you'd rather show up sweating, or in your civvies. Where's *your* team spirit?"

Fergus felt a prickle of guilt. He was thrilled Mum was marrying her boyfriend Jambo and he couldn't have asked for a better stepdad – Jambo loved cycling and football and, what's more, he was a sports reporter for the local paper so he could get Fergus into most matches for nothing. Having to wear these ridiculous clothes felt like a step too far, though.

But if it made Mum happy . . .

"We're only joking," he said, nudging Daisy. "They're . . . brilliotic."

"Beast!" she agreed quickly, trying not to catch sight of herself.

Mum looked at them all trying to be happy for her – and not making a very good job of it. She laughed. "Och, I know you're only being nice," she said. "And you're right. None of you look like . . . you." She turned to the shop assistant.

"We'll go and have a think about it. The big day's still a few months away, after all."

Fergus sighed with relief as he slipped back into his jeans and t-shirt. A lot could happen in a few months – the Internationals for a start. The team had been training hard and, since Mum's friend Charlie had worked her magic getting them all to bond as well as work beyond their comfort zones in the Wreck-it Run, they'd really been racking up top-notch timings.

"I can't wait to get back on the track," said Daisy, as they all wandered back up Princess Street. "Last session Wesley said he's going to help me with a tighter turn, and Minnie said she'd teach Belinda to bunny hop."

Fergus grinned. "Who'd have thought it back when we were on opposing teams?" he said.

"And long may the truce continue," added Grandpa. "The last thing I want is to go back to all that fussing and fighting. Save your grudges for the real rivals at Manchester."

At that, Fergus felt a swirl of something in his tummy, like a crackle of electricity or the flap of a butterfly. Daisy turned to him, eyes wide, and he knew she could feel it too: hope, that's what it was, and possibility, and, most of all, team spirit. So, with that filling their heads and hearts, the friends bounded back along Napier Street and up the steps to the flat.

"Jambo," called Fergus as he burst through the door. "You won't believe what Mum made us put on! It was worse than –"

He stopped when he saw his soon-to-be-stepdad sitting at the table, a letter open in front of him, and a frown on his face deeper than the Firth of Forth. "What's up?" Fergus asked. "Has something happened?"

"It's from the International Cycling Board," said Daisy, eyeing the logo on the letter. "Isn't it?"

"Aye," Jambo nodded. "It is. And no, nothing's happened. At least not yet." He looked up as Grandpa came puffing through the door, helping Mum with the shopping. "It's here," he said.

"What's here?" asked Fergus, exasperated now. "Tell us!"

"Yes, tell us!" agreed Daisy. "Are the Internationals off? Are we disqualified?"

"Have they moved them to Timbuctoo?" tried Fergus.

"No, no, no." Jambo shook his head. "It's nothing that bad. It's just . . . "

"The team," Grandpa interrupted. "They want to know, don't they?"

"Want to know what?" chorused Fergus and Daisy loudly.

Jambo looked at Grandpa, then back at the kids. "Who's on the team," he said.

Grandpa frowned. "And who's off."

Falling Off and Falling Out

"They need to know the names of the four team members," Grandpa explained to the squad as they assembled at Middlebank. "We've been training as a squad, but now we need to put forward our best four for the competition."

"Just four?" Calamity asked, confused.

"And two substitutes," Grandpa added quickly. "So even if you don't make the starting line-up, there's everything to play for."

"But . . . " Minnie did the maths. "That still means two of us are left out."

"Not left out," Grandpa said. "The whole squad will have a part to play. We'll need everyone for support."

"Support?" scoffed Wesley. "Well it won't be me sitting on the sidelines."

"Or me," said his sidekick, Dermot.

"It had better not be any of my boys," blustered Wesley's dad and team coach Choppy Wallace.

"Or your girls," Belinda pointed out crossly.

Choppy reddened. "Of course, of course," he replied. "What I mean is, my lot all deserve to go through."

Wesley, Mikey, Belinda and Dermot all nodded furiously.

"What about us?" demanded Daisy, crossing her arms. "We all deserve it too, don't we?"

Fergus, Minnie and Calamity crossed their arms to show they agreed.

"And we're the original Hercules' Hopefuls," Calamity pointed out. "That's got to stand for something."

Fergus looked at Grandpa hopefully. He had to be on the team, surely? So his times had been down a bit compared to Wesley lately, but he'd been the fastest in the Nationals by far.

But nothing, it seemed, was certain anymore.

"It doesn't matter which team you were on to start with," Grandpa told them. "You're all on the same squad now.

And the truth is, we don't know who's going through to the final team, not yet."

Fergus felt his stomach sink, and could see from Daisy's face that she was none too pleased either. "It'll be fine," he whispered. "We'll both get on the team, I know it."

"You heard Herc," Daisy hissed back. "He doesn't know who's on and who's off. No one does."

Fergus knew she was right, but he had to believe they'd both make it. They'd been together from before the team had even got together – he'd helped Daisy build her first bike! – and leaving one of them out was unthinkable.

"The fact is, you've all got great strengths," explained Grandpa. "Wesley and Fergus are fantastically fast and almost neck and neck for times. Daisy

14

and Dermot have stamina and are determined. Belinda and Minnie make a formidable partnership. And Calamity and Mikey always manage to surprise us with last-minute magic."

"So what do you propose, Herc?" asked Choppy. "Tossing a coin?"

"Drawing straws?" mumbled Mikey.

"Picking names out of a hat?" moaned Minnie.

Grandpa shook his head in astonishment. "We're not playing party games," he pointed out. "This is a serious cycling situation, so there's only one way to sort it out."

"What's that then?" demanded Daisy.

Grandpa smiled. "By bike, of course."

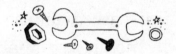

Of course this was fair, Fergus said to himself as the eight of them checked their helmets and slipped into their saddles for a warm-up session. And he had nothing to worry about, not really. He'd put in good races, and so would Daisy and the others. Grandpa was right, there were six places on the team, if you counted the reserves. And, even though the thought of not making the starting line-up was terrible, he probably could live with being a reserve. Especially as it would almost certainly be two of Wallace's lot being left out!

"We'll not be timing you today," Grandpa announced. "That'll come at the weekend when we run our three events: a knock-out race of Devil Takes the Hindmost, a Keirin, and a road race."

"Why three?" asked Mikey.

"Yes, why not just a straight time trial?" added Minnie.

"Because the coaches need to see different skills over distance and at a sprint," said Daisy, rolling her eyes. "Obviously."

"Now, now," said Grandpa. "No need to be narky. But yes, that's right. The Internationals will be run over three races so we need to get the right balance."

"But no slacking," warned Choppy. "Because we'll be watching you all the way."

Fine by me, thought Fergus, as the team headed out to the track. They were used to this by now – all working together to make sure everyone got a chance to ride the slipstream then speed ahead, all taking turns in first place. But, this time, as they lined up, Fergus felt a strange tension in the air, and felt his bike wobble as Wesley nudged him out of the way.

"This is my place," Wesley said. "Inside track, everyone knows that."

Fergus budged over to let Wesley in. No point in fighting, this was only a warm-up, after all. And what had Charlie taught them? That this was all about fun, not fighting. He'd try to remember that and he hoped Wesley would do the same.

But after a few laps, things hadn't improved. If anything they'd got much, much worse, and not just between him and Wesley: Minnie and Mikey weren't talking after she'd alleyooped in front of her brother, sending him off track and into the grass;

Belinda had accused Calamity of sabotage for swerving into her; Calamity claimed Dermot had stopped dead deliberately, making him swerve in the first place; and as for Daisy, she was furious with Fergus for pipping her at the post on a sprint. Even though he'd tried to say sorry she'd stomped off in a sulk.

"Och, it'll be fine," Grandpa assured Fergus as he slid off his bike in a sweat.

"You're a team – on and off the track. You'll get through this, just like you all got through the Highland Head-to-head when Wesley's lot got lost in the mountains. Remember the Wreck-it Run? You hated that to begin with but it all came together in the end."

As Fergus wheeled his bike slowly towards home, he remembered the race round the hospital track, on the kart he and Daisy had designed together. They hadn't won – they'd been beaten by Morgan and her sister Sorcha, Fergus's brand-new best friend (after Daisy, of course) – but they hadn't let that get them down. If anything, that was the race that had brought them all together.

"We'll be fine," he said to Chimp, repeating Grandpa's words. "Team spirit. That's what it's all about."

Chimp barked a happy reply and Fergus found himself smiling at the dog's confidence. But, as he looked back to see his friends scattering their separate ways, and Daisy speeding off across the common, he wasn't so sure Chimp, or he, was right.

He wasn't sure the team spirit was strong enough.

Or if he'd been a fool to believe in it at all.

Trouble Off the Track

By mid-morning the next day, Fergus had serious doubts. By the afternoon, he knew he'd been right: the team spirit was gone.

It had started when he'd gone for a quick spin on Carnoustie Common ahead of practice. "Just to get the muscles warm and working," he'd said when Grandpa asked where he was off to.

"Are you meeting Daisy?" Grandpa asked him.

Fergus shook his head. "She's out. I left a message with Mrs D, but you know what she's like at passing those on."

Grandpa laughed. "Worried you'll be up for corrupting her!" he said. "As if a ride round the park just the pair of you could be a problem. And Mrs MacCafferty'll be there to keep an eye on you anyway, I'll warrant."

Chimp gave a yelp at the mention of Mrs MacCafferty, whose cat Carol was his arch-nemesis.

Fergus shrugged. "If Daisy calls back tell her I'll see her there."

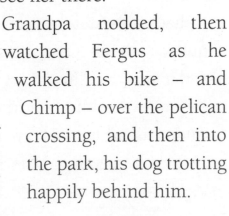

Grandpa nodded, then watched Fergus as he walked his bike – and Chimp – over the pelican crossing, and then into the park, his dog trotting happily behind him.

"Safe as houses," Grandpa said to himself, and got back to polishing some new brake calipers he'd just taken off an old Sullivan Swift.

Out on the common, as he cycled at a steady pace round the old cinder track he'd helped to build, Fergus felt someone's eyes on him. Skidding to a sudden halt, he turned to see a patch of peonies twitch and a familiar head disappear behind an enormous blue flower.

"Wesley?" he called. "Is that you?"

"No," came the reply. "It's definitely Dermot."

"Yeah, Dermot," someone echoed.

Fergus bristled. He knew when he was being lied to, and spied on. He had an idea, and picked up a stick.

"Fetch!" he called to Chimp, and threw it straight into the flower patch.

Chimp, who had been busy burying a stone, lifted his head, saw the stick, and ran pell-mell into the peonies, barking for all he was worth. "Any minute . . . now!" Fergus said to himself, as Wesley and Dermot came yelping onto the track, chased by a merry mongrel who clearly felt he deserved a reward for finding not just an old twig, but two twits besides.

Fergus sighed at the sorry sight of his team-mates. "Spying, were we?" he asked.

"So what if we were?" said Wesley. "No law against that."

"I suppose," said Fergus. "But it's not very sporting, is it? Not against your own team."

"Every little helps," said Wesley. "If I can work out how to take one second off you, then who cares how I did it?"

"Yeah, who cares?" repeated Dermot.

"I care," Fergus said. "And I bet the others do too."

Wesley arched an eyebrow. "Oh, I wouldn't be so sure about that," he smirked.

An hour later, Fergus didn't know which was worse – the mess the squad was in, or the fact Wesley had been right. First Minnie had refused to teach

Belinda how to bunny hop, so Belinda said she'd get her dad to see Minnie didn't make the team, as his company Bruce's Biscuits was the Hercules' Hopefuls squad sponsor. Then Calamity complained that Mikey was making faces at him to put him off.

"It's just my normal face!" Mikey protested.

"More's the pity," replied his sister Minnie.

But, worst of all, Daisy was in another horrible huff because she found out Fergus had been practising without her.

"I left a message with your mum," he insisted.

"You might be lying," Daisy replied.

"I never lie!" Fergus said. "You know that."

Daisy paused. Then she sighed. "I know," she said quietly. "I'm sorry."

"It's okay," Fergus said. "This test has got everyone on tenterhooks. I'm terrified."

Daisy smiled. "Me too! Why don't I come over for tea and we can go through manoeuvres?"

"That'd be brilliotic!" Fergus began. But then he remembered something. "You don't mind if Sorcha is there, do you? We've arranged to hang out."

Daisy's jaw set and her face flushed red. "Oh, forget it," she snapped. "You're obviously busy with your *new* friend."

Fergus flinched. Sorcha loved sport almost as much as he did, so he did spend a lot of time with her. But that didn't mean he'd replaced Daisy. "Sorcha's away tomorrow, you could come over then instead," he suggested, a touch of sorrow in his voice. "Or, better, we could *all* be friends together? I'm sure Sorcha would be happy to talk tactics with us."

But Daisy's mind was made up. "I'll see you in the morning for the Devil Takes the Hindmost," she said crossly. "Or rather, you'll see my dust."

"Daisy!" Grandpa said, surprised.

Fergus opened his mouth to say something but nothing came out.

"If the wind changes, you'll stay like that," Wesley said.

"Oh, whatever," Fergus snapped, finally finding his words.

"Fergus!" Grandpa scolded. "If your mam heard you say that, she'd have a conniption."

Fergus sighed. "I'm sorry," he said.

And he was, truly sorry. But as he cycled slowly home, Grandpa and Chimp following him, he couldn't help feeling that choosing the team might mean the end of it as well.

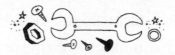

"I think you're imagining things," said Mum, as she plopped pizza onto Sorcha's plate. Sorcha gave her a thumbs up in reply, and Mum smiled and signed, "You're welcome," back.

"I'm not," Fergus replied, slipping a sliver of pizza under the table to a waiting Chimp. "It's all gone wrong."

Sorcha pulled the pen and paper she always carried out of her pocket and scribbled something down before pushing it over to Fergus.

Fergus was learning to use sign language, but it was taking time, and the notebook was the only way for the two of them to talk properly right now. He grabbed the paper.

Focus on the race. That's all you can do for now.

"Focus on the race," he read out loud. "That's all you can do for now."

"Wise words," Grandpa told Sorcha. "Fancy a job as assistant coach?"

Sorcha nodded eagerly, then grabbed the pad and wrote another note. Grandpa laughed then read it out loud.

Not sure Dermot and Wesley are clever enough to learn sign language, though.

"Too stubborn more like," said Fergus, who found himself smiling, despite himself. Sorcha was right. He had to focus on what he *could* do: ride. The others would settle down once everything was decided. And, as for Daisy, she was a cert for the team, and she'd come round; she was his best friend after all. And with that thought a happy seed in his head, he let himself feel excitement for the first time. Tomorrow was race day, and he was going to ride for all he was worth.

Devil Take the Hindmost

As his team-mates wheeled up beside him on the starting line, Fergus gave Daisy a nod of encouragement. But all he got back was a steely glare. *She's just focusing*, he told himself. *Same as me.* And he adjusted his helmet one last time for good measure.

"Listen up, Hopefuls!" Grandpa called the team to attention. "This morning's race is Devil Take the Hindmost. It will test your stamina, speed and tactics!"

"My favourite," whispered Wesley. "Sudden death for the slowcoaches."

"Mine too," said Belinda. "Gets the track nice and clear for us frontrunners."

Fergus felt himself shiver. This was crazy. It was no more scary than any other race, despite the name, so why was his heart pounding so much? He glanced over at Daisy for some reassurance but she was already low over her handlebars, eyes on the track.

"You know the rules," continued Choppy. "Four laps, and the last one past the finishing line each lap has to drop out."

"That will give us a leaderboard as we head into the Keirin this afternoon," said Grandpa. "The four who make it round every lap will give us a top four to beat."

"And four losers," Wesley whispered again.

"I heard that," Grandpa said.

Wesley shrugged. "Well, it's true."

Grandpa looked at Choppy for back-up but Choppy was busy polishing his puncture repair kit, pretending not to notice.

"Can we just get on with it?" asked Calamity. "I'll topple off if I don't get started soon."

Grandpa sighed. It was true the gangly champion was better at high speed than staying still. "Fine," he replied. "On your marks . . . "

Fergus leaned forward, like Daisy next to him, poised with his right foot on the pedal, ready for a strong off.

"Get set . . . "

Fergus took a deep breath, and reminded himself of Sorcha's words. *Focus*, he said to himself. *It'll all come good.*

"And GO!" yelled Grandpa.

And GO is exactly what they did, pushing off in unison and pulling away in one sleek, practised pack.

Off to a flying start, Fergus spun over the smooth concrete, legs pumping, heart hammering. He was neck and neck with Daisy, pedalling in perfect unison right-left, right-left, as they took the first turn. It was as if they were one, as if they could hear each other's thoughts and sense each other's movements. *Even if she's not speaking to me*, Fergus said to himself as he kept time for the second turn in a row.

Next to her, Wesley was inching forward, with Minnie and Belinda level just millimetres behind. Dermot and Mikey were already trailing a little. But Calamity, who'd got a wobbly start, was really flagging at the back, and was the first to fall when the whistle blew for Lap One.

"One down, three to go," yelled Wesley as Calamity pulled on the brakes and off the track. But his words caught on the wind, and besides, his fellow racers had eyes and ears for one thing and one thing only: the finish. And so they spun on into a second lap, led by Wesley, Belinda and Minnie, Fergus and Daisy in fourth place, and Mikey and Dermot now fighting it out for fifth.

The whistle blew again, and this time it was Dermot's turn to pull off the track. The next lap, Mikey was gone too.

Wesley was still leading the pack, Belinda and Minnie chasing. Fergus and Daisy were neck and neck just behind them.

"Maybe Daisy and I can both be fourth," Fergus said to himself. "Then Grandpa'll have to let us both on the team!" And the thought was so good and so strong, he felt sure Daisy must have sensed it, and be feeling it too as they turned into the final straight.

"Nice one, Dais," he said, out loud this time.

"Thanks," she said, without a flicker of a smile, and promptly pulled forward, crossing the line level with Belinda and Minnie, leaving a befuddled Fergus in fifth place, and out of the race.

Pulling off the track to join Calamity, Mikey and Dermot, Fergus watched from the sidelines, stunned, as the final four rode to the coaches and Choppy called the placings: "In first place, my Wesley, and rightly so."

Fergus rolled his eyes, like he and Daisy always did, and looked at her to see if she was doing the same too. But Daisy was concentrating on Choppy.

"In joint second place, Belinda Bruce and Minnie McLeod," he continued. "And in fourth place, Daisy Devlin."

Fergus could see Daisy's heart swell with pride, and he wished she could see his was doing the same too. Even though he'd lost. Even though he had an inkling Daisy had *deliberately* knocked him out. Even though he'd really have to pull his socks up for the Keirin.

But Daisy didn't look at him, and, as they headed back to the changing rooms for juice and sandwiches, Fergus couldn't help feel he was in danger of losing not just a place on the team, but a friend as well.

The Keirin

Lunch in the locker room was usually a celebration, with Grandpa and Choppy going through team tactics while Fergus and his friends shared stories and jokes as well as their crisps. But today, not even cold sausage sandwiches could cheer Fergus up.

Not only had he performed badly in the first race, but he'd never even ridden a Keirin before, and wished he could discuss tactics with Daisy but she was obviously ignoring him. "I don't just need to pull my socks up," he mumbled to Chimp. "I need to pull a rabbit out of a hat."

Chimp yapped at the word "rabbit" and again at the sausage sandwich dangling from Fergus's fingers.

"Are you not eating that?" Calamity asked.

Fergus shook his head. "Not that hungry," he said. "D'you want it?" He held it out to Calamity.

Calamity nodded and snaffled it quick before Chimp could get a chance.

"You'll wish you'd eaten that later," said Daisy. "You need to keep your strength up."

Fergus looked over in surprise. "I – I know," he said, stumbling over his words because he was so pleased Daisy was talking to him again. "Of course you're right."

"Not that I care," she added quickly. "Means I've got a better chance." And she took a bite out of her banana.

Fergus felt his happiness slip again, and a hand on his shoulder. "Och, she doesn't mean it." Grandpa had obviously overheard, but Fergus was glad to hear his reassuring soft voice.

"Doesn't she?" he asked. "It feels like she means every word."

Grandpa shook his head. "Pressure does funny things to people. Things will settle, and you two will be inseparable again. Like peas in a pod, you are."

Fergus smiled weakly. "That's what I thought," he said. "Best friends forever, she said."

"And she'll say it again, mark my words. Here." He handed Fergus another sandwich. "Marmalade. Your favourite. And I'm not taking no for an answer. Daisy was right, you need the energy. And besides, your mum would have my guts for garters if I let you ride on an empty stomach."

Fergus bit into the bittersweet sandwich and forced himself to chew and swallow. Then again. And again. Until he found he did have an appetite after all, and not just for food.

"Ready?" Calamity asked, as he tossed his litter into the bin and missed, twice.

Fergus swallowed his last mouthful and nodded, a rush of energy sending him springing to his feet and raring to go. "Ready!" he replied, then turned to Daisy. "How about you," he tried. "Are you ready?"

"As I'll ever be," she said, looking him straight in the eye without blinking.

Fergus held her gaze as long as he could before turning to Wesley. "Wes?"

Wesley crumpled the wrapper from his flapjack and threw it towards the bin. "Bullseye!" he cried. "I'm on fire. And ready as anything."

Despite everything, Fergus found himself smiling. Competition might be taking its toll right now, but it was what he lived for – the feel of slick tarmac beneath his wheels as he chewed through miles; the cheering of the crowd as he passed them by in a blur;

and, best of all, his team all around him, willing each other on.

He was going to be part of that team, he was sure of it.

"So, the classic Keirin," Choppy began. "My specialty."

"How does it work again?" asked Dermot.

Daisy rolled her eyes and sighed, and Fergus was glad he hadn't been the one to ask after all. "We follow a pacesetter for four laps until they pull off, then we sprint for the finish for a final lap."

"Who?" demanded Wesley. "It had better be someone super speedy."

"Och, it is," replied Grandpa. "It's none other than our very own –"

"Jambo!" Fergus exclaimed, as his stepdad-to-be stepped out of the locker

room, in full team strip, pushing the
second-hand bike Grandpa had done
up for him before their trip to the
Highlands.

"Seriously?" asked Wesley. "But he's
. . . old."

"And a bit . . . well, slow," added
Minnie. "Sorry, Jambo, but you are!"

"Not any more," replied Jambo. "While you lot were all arguing over Charlie, I got on my bike and got practising. I may not be perfect, but I'm better."

"And that's a lesson for us all," added Grandpa.

"Aye," agreed Jambo. "Besides, the first four laps of a Kierin aren't about top speed, they're about going steady. As soon as you see me pull off, then you can really go for it. But not before, you hear?"

Wesley nodded, annoyed.

"First things first, though," Grandpa interrupted before Wesley found something else to complain about. "Take your pick."

And he held out a cycle helmet with slips of paper inside.

"What's that for?" asked Calamity.

Daisy sighed even louder. "We have to draw lots," she said. "To decide lanes."

"Me first!" cried Wesley and grabbed one.

The others dived in behind, each snatching a slip of paper, then unfolding it to find out their fate.

"Lane one for me!" Belinda boasted.

"I'm in five!" wailed Wesley. "I call foul!"

"You can't call foul," said Grandpa. "You picked fair and square. And you went first."

Wesley stomped off to line up as Fergus unfurled the slip of paper in his hand. "3" it said in thick, black pen.

"Lucky you," said Daisy, throwing hers on the floor in disgust.

Fergus picked it up quickly and slipped it in the bin, but not before he'd looked at the number. "8" 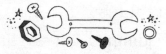 it said. Daisy was looking a bit dejected.

"I'll swap!" Fergus offered. "You can have lane three."

"No," said Daisy. "You heard Herc: I picked fair and square." And she stamped off to the starting line, Fergus following frantically a few paces behind, feeling like he barely even knew Daisy anymore.

"On your marks," called Choppy. "Get set, GO!"

This time, Fergus pushed himself off hard, but made sure not to waste his energy. For the first three laps, it was all about getting up a good pace, and preserving energy for when Jambo made his move to the side. Going into the penultimate lap, he was at the front of the pack, only Minnie and Belinda ahead of him, and Wesley, cycling for his life at his side. He felt safe enough to risk a peek behind, and could see to his joy that Daisy had already sailed past Dermot, who was struggling after his double chocolate fudge slice at lunch, and Calamity and Mikey who were head to head, and, worryingly, almost pedal to pedal. And, it seemed, getting closer.

"Careful!" he heard Grandpa call out from the sidelines, but too late! Fergus heard a massive crash and looked back to see Calamity and Mikey in a tangle on the track. They must have taken out Dermot too, who had landed like a cherry on top of them. But Fergus didn't falter – they were all kitted out, and safe from injury, so he needed to focus on his own race now. "Keep your eyes on the prize!" he heard Grandpa say in his head, and, as Jambo swerved off to the left, leaving the track open for the sprint, that's exactly what Fergus did – he focused on the finish, seeing it in his head as he pumped on the pedals, legs like pistons, lungs fit to burst.

"Come on, Fergie!" he heard Jambo call.

"Sock it to them, Wesley!" Choppy retorted.

"Nice going, Minnie. Give it your all, Belinda!" Grandpa added his voice to the shouts.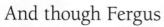

And though Fergus hadn't the air in his lungs to shout himself, he heard the words burst in his head: *Come on, Daisy! You can do it!*

But as he sailed across the finish line in third place, Wesley and Minnie taking first and second, he turned to see not Daisy, but Belinda fly into fourth place, leaving his best friend fuming in fifth.

"Dais!" he cried, as she fled from the track. "Daisy, come back!"

"Leave her," Grandpa said, coming to congratulate him. "It's fifth, not bottom – it was a fine result. Anyway, after this morning's knock-out race it puts the

55

pair of you nice and even for the road race tomorrow."

"I know but –"

"Butts are for sitting on." Grandpa grinned. "Isn't that what Daisy would say?"

"I suppose," said Fergus.

But he didn't think she'd be thinking that right now.

In fact, for the first time ever, he didn't have a clue what Daisy might be thinking. And that made him sadder than ever.

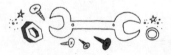

"Mum," he began when he walked sorrowfully through the door of the flat. "You won't believe –"

"Not now, Fergus, love," Mum warned, standing on a chair while Mrs MacCafferty pinned white taffeta into place. "I'm otherwise occupied."

"Is that . . . ?"

"Aye," Mum replied. "So you'd best run and tell Jambo to stay out if he knows what's good for him. It's bad luck for him to see the dress."

Fergus nodded, "Course," he said. Then, "You look beautiful, Mum" he added, as he was about to slip out.

"Och, away with you!" Mum laughed, but Fergus could see from her smile that she'd liked it.

He caught Jambo putting his bike away downstairs.

"Och aye, serious business, this wedding dress," Jambo said, winking.

57

"I'll be off down the shop for a pint of milk then. Coming?"

Fergus opened his mouth to say yes when he had a thought: he needed advice and Grandpa was off with Choppy, sorting out the route for tomorrow's road race, Mum was too busy with the wedding, Sorcha was away, and as for Daisy – well, she was the trouble he needed to talk about. Jambo was great, but there was only one person Fergus really wanted to talk to, and only one place he could go.

"No, you're all right," he told Jambo. "I'll see you later."

Once Jambo was safely round the corner of Napier Street, Fergus whispered to Chimp, "Fancy a little ride?"

All's Fair

Whomp!

The bike landed with an expert thud right in front of the Palace Pedallers' track. Fergus grinned to himself: he was getting good at this – all he had to do was get up to speed on his bike, imagine where in Nevermore he wanted to be, backpedal three times, and hey presto! Peering at the palava playing out in front of him, however, he wasn't so sure he'd made the right choice.

Hector Hamilton, King Woebegot and Unlucky Luke's dad, Percy the court wizard (otherwise known as Percy the Pretty Useless) seemed to be locked in a shouting match. Unlucky Luke, Princess Lily, Prince Waldorf, Dimmock and Scary Mary watched agape from the sidelines.

"What in the name of Waltzing Matilda is going on?" asked a familiar Aussie dog.

Fergus looked down at Chimp, surprised to see him sitting with his paws on his hips . . . surprised he even had hips! "I don't know," he sighed. "But I think we'd better find out."

As the pair pedalled closer to the podium, they could see the king's face getting redder and redder, and Fergus's dad getting paler and paler, while the wizard stood between them looking worried.

"I'm right!" yelled the king.

"No, I'm right," insisted Hector. "It's wrong."

"Oh, do make up your minds about what's wrong and what's not," pleaded Percy. "The spells won't make themselves."

"Unfortunately," muttered Prince Waldorf. "They'd probably do a better job."

"Oh, do shut up," Princess Lily said crossly. "Dad's wrong, it's not right, and that's the end of it."

"End of what?" asked Fergus, more perplexed than ever.

"Fergie!" Lily cried. "About time. Perhaps you can talk some sense into my dad."

"About what?" Fergus asked. "What's wrong? And what's right? And what's this about spells?"

"Waldorf and Lily's dad wants *my* dad to use spells against the Darklands Demons in the first race this afternoon," explained Unlucky Luke. "But *your* dad says that's wrong."

"Which is right!" said Lily. "Isn't it, Mary?"

Scary Mary said nothing but nodded quickly. Team member number three of the Palace Pedallers was very shy.

"Well, if spells mean we beat Cousin Derek and his team then I say we use every weapon we've got," Waldorf announced.

"That's my boy," said the king, puffed up with pride.

Fergus shook his head. "Dad's right," he said. "It's cheating. Wouldn't you feel rotten if you won knowing it was down to spells, not skills?"

Waldorf shrugged. "A win's a win," he said.

Hector Hamilton shook his head. "I'm the one with the coach's cap," Fergus's dad said. "And I set the rules."

"And I'm the one with the crown," retorted King Woebegot. "And I'm the one who can lock you back up in the Dungeon of Despair if I feel like it."

"Ha!" said Waldorf, delighted. "We win!"

"Hector?" begged Lily, looking imploring at Fergus's dad.

Fergus crossed his fingers. Chimp crossed his paws. But deep down, they knew they were fighting a losing battle.

And so did Hector. "Fine," he said. "Have it your way. But don't say I didn't warn you. And don't expect me to congratulate you if you win by foul means, not fair."

"Fair?" spluttered King Woebegot. "Duke Dastardly of the Darklands wouldn't know fair if it hit him in the face with a kipper."

"Nor would Prince Derek," added Waldorf.

"So, crank up the cauldron." The king grinned at Percy. "Spells it is!"

"This," whispered Lily to Fergus as they set off for a warm-up lap, "is going to go horribly wrong."

"I think you might be right," replied Fergus. But he held out his hand for their special finger-wiggling handshake to show he was on her side.

To his delight, she wiggled her fingers right back. "Friends first and forever," she said and winked.

"First and forever?" he asked.

"It's our new team motto," she said. "Your dad's idea. To remind us what's most important. Do you like it?"

Fergus thought about Daisy and his mates back home, and the team here too. "First and forever," he said, nodding. "I like it. I like it a lot."

"What? So *we* don't actually get to do any spells?" asked Waldorf, clearly disappointed.

"No, no and no again!" blustered Percy the Pretty Useless, brandishing his wand in one hand and a bottle of fizzing purple potion in the other. "You're not licensed to handle this kind of . . . special equipment."

"And you are?" yelled Waldorf.

"I've got my Level Seven Wizard Skills diploma, I'll have you know," boasted Percy.

"It's true," said Luke.

"Level seven out of how many?" demanded Waldorf. He turned to Luke. "You gave your son chicken feet and bear claws."

"Well, yes, but . . . but that's not the point," stuttered Percy. "The point is, I'll do my magic –"

"And you lot concentrate on your bikes," Fergus interrupted.

"Aye," Hector backed his son up. "You heard the lad. Just carry on doing what you do best."

"We will," promised Lily, snapping the strap on her helmet. "Won't we, Pedallers?"

Mary nodded in agreement, while Luke looked up from adjusting his specially adapted pedals. "Definitely," he said.

"Waldorf?" asked Fergus.

"I suppose," said the prince, reluctantly. "Though I don't see what it's got to do with you."

"Assistant coach," said Hector, putting his arm round his son. "Isn't that right?"

Fergus felt himself flush with pride. "Beast!" he said.

"What am I then?" demanded Chimp.

Fergus looked his dog up and down and clocked the spanner sticking out of his pocket. "Head mechanic," he decided. "Right, Dad?"

"Right," agreed Hector.

"Have you lot quite finished?" the king said. "Because that wretched duke and his Darklands lot are here and the quicker we can trick them, the quicker I can win back the fifty groats he owes me from that snail race thirty-seven years ago."

Fergus glanced over at Duke Dastardly and his team, who had assembled on the trackside. The duke was a tall, glowering man, with a coat as black as night and a hat that looked like it was made out of dead ravens. He shuddered.

"Oh, you'll win," said Lily. "But by pedal power."

"I don't care how you do it," snapped

the king. "Just get on with it. The queen's already got a headache and you know what she's like when she's in a mood."

Fergus gulped. As if the duke wasn't bad enough, they had Queen Woebegot to contend with as well. She was rather too fond of yelling "Orf with his head!" when she was cross. He hoped she didn't shout that one out today; not even against Prince Derek. Anything might happen if Percy was in charge of the spells. Fergus looked at the Duke's son lining up with his teammates – Norman, Norris and Nigel, according to the team sheet – all equally pale and grim-faced. Derek was fast, faster than Lily even, so this was going to be one tough race, magic or not.

Pedalling Pandemonium

"Orn your marks . . . " called Queen Woebegot haughtily. "Get set . . . and tally ho!"

Fergus held his breath as the teams lurched off down the first straight. He wasn't used to seeing the race from the coach's position. It was all he could do not to run out onto the track – now he understood how hard Grandpa and Choppy must find it standing on the sidelines. Then a terrible thought occurred to him: what if he didn't make the final team for the Internationals? He'd be stuck in this spot back in Scotland as well.

"Don't," warned Chimp. "I know what you're thinking, and it's not going to help."

"So you're psychic as well as a chatterbox?" said Fergus.

"I can fix a sprocket, sing a lullaby and dance the cha-cha-cha," said Chimp. "But I don't like to boast."

Fergus was about to ask his dog to prove it when he heard a cry of "Abracadabra!" coming from Percy next to him. The king, sitting behind them, cheered as a swarm of very cross wasps shot out of nowhere and swarmed after Prince Derek.

"Help!" cried the prince, swatting one from his visor and swerving from side to side to get away from them.

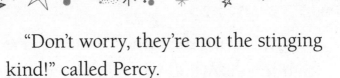

"Don't worry, they're not the stinging kind!" called Percy.

"How thoughtful," said Fergus.

"Actually, it's because I haven't worked that bit out yet," admitted Percy quietly. "But they're still scary, hey?"

"Cheaters!" yelled Duke Dastardly, and nudged a small man in a spangly cloak standing next to him.

The small man waved a wand and sparks shot out. Then a frog the size of a cow appeared on the track, unrolled a long sticky tongue, and licked the wasps into oblivion.

"Holy mackerel!" yelped Chimp.

"No," said Percy. "Horrible Higgins. The Duke's own wizard and my arch-rival."

"Orf with his head!" screeched the queen, though it wasn't clear if she meant the giant frog or the wizard.

Fergus watched, horrified, as Mary's front wheel got stuck on the frog and she flew over the handlebars, landing with a squelch.

"Help!" she mouthed silently as the frog began to unfurl its enormous tongue towards Mary herself.

"Don't you dare!" roared Cook, Mary's terrifying mother who was watching from the other side of the tracks.

"I'll fix that!" cried Percy and let loose a shower of green flashes that rained down on the frog, dissolving it into a puddle of goop, and setting Mary free, although she was a little sticky.

"What was that?" demanded Fergus.

"Glue remover," said Percy. "Obviously."

"Well, good," said Hector. "But can you stop now and just let my team get on with cycling?"

Fergus glanced at the pack – in the lead, Waldorf was head to head with Norman, followed by Lily and Luke battling it out with Norris and Nigel. The sticky Mary and a scowling Derek were bringing up the rear, working hard to catch up.

"Come on, Pedallers," Hector yelled. "Eyes on the prize!"

But before Fergus could add anything about staying long and low, or keeping elbows in, a lightning flash lit up the track, and a two-headed serpent (one lion, one crocodile) appeared on the podium right in front of Queen Woebegot.

"Orf with its heads!" she yelled.

Hector turned to Percy. "You promised to stop!" he pointed out.

"It wasn't me!" replied the wizard. "It was Horrible Higgins! But this . . . " He waved his wand " . . . is all my own work." And with that he conjured up a four-headed serpent (one lion, one crocodile, one fanged baboon, and one, rather surprisingly, poodle) to eat the two-headed one. "Take that!" he cried.

"How dare you!" sniped Duke Dastardly, nudging Horrible Higgins, who immediately conjured up a six-headed serpent to eat the four-headed one, this time with added vampire bat, and, worse, a cat that looked alarmingly like Carol.

Chimp yelped.

The queen screamed, "Orf with all their heads!" and promptly fainted.

"Och, for heaven's sake," cried Hector as Percy lifted his wand again.

"Stop!" cried Fergus. "Please. What about the race?"

"The race?" said a voice. "Oh, we won that about two minutes ago. Or rather, Luke did. He's used to dealing with this sort of tomfoolery."

Fergus's mouth fell open as he saw Lily unclip her helmet, followed by a beaming Waldorf, Luke and Mary.

"But . . . " he blustered. "How . . . ?"

"Oh, you can't let a little fighting distract you," said Lily, looking her dad right in the eye, who reddened as the duke paled. "Not when there's something serious at stake."

"Is this true?" demanded Duke Dastardly, grasping Prince Derek by the collar. "You lost?"

Derek yanked himself free. "Yes, but only because of your stupid magic tricks," he said. "If you'd left it to me, we'd have beaten them easily." And with a flick of his fringe, he stomped off to the hover van, followed by Nigel, Norris and Norman.

The duke turned to the king. "Best of three, eh, Kevin?"

King Woebegot nodded. "If you say so, Dave."

A thin smile flickered on Duke

Dastardly's narrow face. "We'll get you next time," he seethed, then stalked off too, whispering to Horrible Higgins as he went.

"Well, thank heavens that's all over," said the queen. "Having the other side of the family over is always so trying."

"Well, only two more to go," said Fergus's dad, then turned to the king. "But no more magic tricks!"

"It was way too dangerous," said Fergus.

"And we didn't need them anyway," added Lily.

"Fine, fine," said the king, slapping at a leftover wasp who was licking his shoe. "No tricks. Unless they try one first."

"Not even if they try one first!" snapped Lily, a bit cross her parents had missed her victory because they were distracted by wizard wars.

King Woebegot sighed and nodded. "Time for tea?" he said. "There's scones."

"And jam," said the queen. "As long as Cook's made some. If not, orf with her head, I say!"

Mary looked more scared than ever.

"Don't worry," whispered Lily. "She never really means it."

"Coming, Fergus?" asked Dad, as everyone set off for the castle.

Fergus shook his head. "I need to get back," he said. "Got some fighting of my own to sort out."

Dad nodded. "I've got every confidence in you, son. You showed today you know what matters most to a team."

Fergus nodded as he felt his chest puff with pride again, "Thanks, Dad." It was true, he felt as if he could handle his own problems himself now, without needing to ask for help.

"See you soon, though, eh?" Dad said, then added, "I suppose you're too big for a hug now?"

Fergus shook his head. "Never." And he let his dad pull him in for a squeeze before he headed off after the others to the castle.

Lily had lingered behind. "I'd better go," she said. "Or it'll be my head Mother wants offing."

"See you soon," said Fergus.

Lily grasped his hand then, wiggling her fingers. "Friends first and forever," she said.

"Exactly," he said, wiggling back. "Everyone could do with remembering that."

"What about me?" demanded Chimp. "Don't I deserve a secret handshake?"

Lily laughed and took a paw; Fergus did the same. "Friends first and forever!" they chorused.

Fergus smiled to himself. *Now I just need to convince Daisy of that,* he thought.

"Good luck with that, mate," said Chimp, reading his thoughts.

Road Rage

Fergus's tummy was alive with butterflies as he arrived at Carnoustie Common to find the leader board up. Wesley, Minnie and Belinda were all front of the pack, and his name in joint fourth place with Daisy. *So I need to come at least third to be guaranteed a place,* Fergus thought. But then so did Daisy. And if Calamity or Dermot did really well they might still beat them both.

"Today's not going to be easy,"

Grandpa said, as Fergus clipped on his helmet and checked his elbow pads. "But I know you've got what it takes."

"What's that?" Fergus asked.

"Commitment," said Grandpa. "Determination. And a wee drop of talent too, of course."

But hadn't they all got that? Fergus looked round at the rest of the squad, each going through their own pre-race ritual: Wesley was doing press-ups, Calamity was trying to touch his toes, Minnie and Mikey were doing a few alleyoops, Belinda was fixing her hair, and Dermot was eating a biscuit. And there was Daisy, who he knew would be reeling off Spokes Sullivan's race times in her head, just like she always did. They were all committed, determined, and though none of them were Spokes, not yet, they all had a wee drop of talent.

Especially Daisy.

"I'll be back in a moment," Fergus said, handing his bike to Grandpa before going over to his friend, who was kneeling by her back tyre, checking the pressure. He crouched down beside her. "Whatever happens," he said, "we'll still be friends, Dais, won't we." He said it so it wasn't a question, so Daisy couldn't say "no".

She looked up, then away again quickly. "Friends," she repeated. "I suppose."

"First and forever, yeah?"

Daisy twisted the cap back on the valve and stood up, so Fergus did the same. "First and forever," she repeated. "If you say so." Then, without even a second glance, she snapped on her helmet, slid onto her saddle, and cycled to the start line, finding a place between Wesley and Minnie.

Fergus sighed. She'd said the words, but it didn't sound like she had meant them, not like Lily. But it was as good as he was going to get, for now. So, with his tummy fluttering, his heart dancing and his fingers crossed, Fergus saddled up and settled into place on the end of the line to listen to Choppy explain the course.

"You're off up Napier Street for a mile, come back down the hill past the Bruce's Biscuits factory, then round the back of the church to end at Middlebank."

"That's . . . miles!" Belinda moaned.

"And uphill too!" added Wesley.

"Aye, it's certainly a tougher run than you'll get on the flat in Manchester at the Internationals," agreed Grandpa. "But if you do well in this, we know you'll do even better at the event. Right, Choppy?"

"Right." Choppy nodded back. "And this morning the roads are closed off to cars for an adult race later, so it's safe, too."

At least our two coaches are getting on today, Fergus thought, and he risked a quick glance at Daisy. And that's when he saw her – looking straight back along the line at him, her eyebrows raised, mirroring his. "She gets it!" he thought to himself. "Beast!" And with that buoying thought, he turned back to the track ahead, and waited for the off.

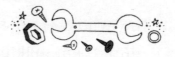

"On your marks . . . " called Choppy. "Get set . . . Go!"

The pack moved off as one, flying along the cinder track, then turning right uphill onto Napier Street. It felt like the Kierin again, all of them keeping pace, right-left, right-left on the pedals, their heads nodding slightly in time with the effort. They were a squad – and a great one, now – no matter who was in the final line-up. They crested the hill, and Fergus felt himself soar inside as they sailed down towards the Bruce's Biscuits factory. There was nothing like that feeling, and he just knew Daisy was feeling it too.

"Come on!" he shouted, to her as much as himself, as they hit the flat for the final mile. "You can do it!"

At that, the whole team seemed to dig deeper, all of them pushing harder, pumping faster, pulling that extra shred of effort from somewhere deep inside. As they headed into Middlebank itself for the last four hundred metres, they began to separate: Wesley, Fergus and Daisy moving ahead, Minnie and Belinda taking the middle, and Calamity, Mikey and Dermot struggling slightly at the back. Sad though he was for his faltering friends, Fergus felt a flood of happiness gush through him at the knowledge that both he and Daisy would make it through.

And that's when he saw it: the flash of a hand-painted sign bouncing up and down saying:

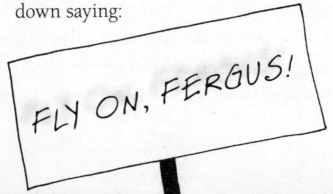

Sorcha's smiling face was bouncing up and down behind it. She flipped the sign round as Fergus sailed past happily and across the finish line. "Daredevil Daisy!" read the other side.

And that's when he heard it: the skid of wheels, and the crunch of a bike hitting the stands. "Daisy!" he yelled out loud, as he turned to see his friend sprawled on the tarmac, the rest of the riders sailing past without stopping, beating her across the finish line, and to a place on the team.

His heart sinking, Fergus dropped his bike, and ran over to help, but Daisy was already scrambling up.

"I'm fine!" she snapped, refusing the hand he'd offered.

But Daisy wasn't fine. She wasn't fine at all. She'd turned away quickly, making a big fuss of picking up her bike, but not before Fergus had seen the hot tears fill her eyes, and her cheeks redden with shame.

"Don't worry, Daisy," he said to her turned back. "Grandpa knows how well you've done. And –" he clutched at his trump card, the one thing that really mattered – "friends first and forever!" he urged her.

But Daisy said nothing. Not then, and not when Grandpa read out the final team line-up: Wesley, Fergus, Minnie and Belinda. Not when Choppy told her she was first reserve, with Calamity second. Not when Mikey and Dermot congratulated her when they themselves were off the team entirely. Not even when Sorcha tried to say sorry, and offered to walk Daisy's bike home for her to save her sore leg.

Sorcha wrote on her pad:

It's my fault, my stupid sign I distracted you.

Daisy shook her head and handed the paper back, then turned to go.

"Look, just wait," Fergus blurted. "I'll talk to Grandpa."

That's when Daisy finally opened her mouth. "If you're going to plead for me, you can stop right now," she said. "It wasn't Sorcha's fault, it was mine. I got distracted, and that's no good. Not in a race. Imagine what it'll be like in the Internationals – TV crews and people cheering. What if I get distracted then?"

Fergus shrugged.

"Then we'll all lose, that's what, and it'll be down to me."

"But –" began Fergus. Then he remembered what Daisy always said. "Butts are for sitting on," he said, hoping to raise a smile.

But Daisy just rolled her eyes. "Whatever," she said.

And with that, she was gone.

So as the rest of the team wheeled their bikes away and seemed to settle their scores – whooping over their places, tossing coins over shirt numbers, and arguing whether Chimp or Dermot should be team mascot – all Fergus could think about was Daisy: all the amazing times they'd had racing side by side; all the times they'd known just what each other was thinking. Now they were places and poles apart, and he realised he'd never felt so lost in his life.

Friends First and Forever

It was Saturday a week later and Fergus and Daisy still hadn't made up. She'd ignored him at school, walking home with a new boy in their class, Will Schofield, who seemed really nice but who Daisy hadn't even spoken to before that week. She'd ignored Fergus at practice, helping Wesley out instead. That had really hurt Fergus's feelings. And she'd ignored the text he'd sent her that morning from Mum's phone, asking if she wanted to come over for tea.

"What do you think?" Mum said, flicking through a cake catalogue on the sofa, Chimp drooling happily on her lap. "A Triple-filled Profiterole Tower or a Chocolate Cherry Extravaganza?"

"Whatever," Fergus mumbled.

"Fergie!" Jambo warned. "I know it's only cake, but . . . cake matters!"

"I'm sorry," Fergus said, and he meant it. It was just so hard concentrating on the wedding, and even on the Internationals, without Daisy by his side. "Maybe the —"

But he didn't finish his sentence because Mum's phone beeped and he lunged to pick it up.

"From Daisy?" Mum asked hopefully.

Fergus clicked, scrolled through and sighed. "Sorcha," he said. "She wants to know if I can go over and watch the Spokes race later."

"Of course you can," said Mum. "If you'd like to."

Fergus thought. He *would* like to go over to Sorcha's. But not without Daisy. He'd not seen a single Spokes race without her reeling off stats at his side, not celebrated a single Spokes win without Daisy cheering with him.

Then it came to him. "Maybe," he replied, to Mum.

And to Sorcha he wrote: *Thanks, but there's something else I have to do today.*

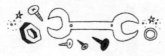

Fergus had never been as nervous as he was when he knocked on Daisy's door that afternoon. "Daft," he told himself. "It's only Daisy."

But Daisy wasn't "only" anything. She was everything, and Fergus had realised he'd do anything to make sure she knew that. When she opened the door, he thrust the package into her hand before she could slam it or say a word. "Here," he said. "Open it."

To his astonishment, Daisy did as he'd asked, pulled the poster from its tube, and unrolled it. "I don't believe it. Your signed Spokes poster?" she said in

awe. "Hang on." Then, to Fergus's even greater astonishment, she handed him a package of her own from by the front door. "Here," she said. "Your turn."

Fergus unwrapped the oblong parcel carefully, running his finger along the tape so as not to tear the paper, then peeling it back to reveal his present. "Your *Cycling Times* signed by Spokes!" he exclaimed.

The pair looked at each other, smiles

slowly spreading across their faces until Fergus felt his own stretch so wide it almost hurt. "Friends?" he said.

Daisy grinned back. "First and forever," she finished. "And I'm sorry I nearly messed that up. I was just cross with myself and you being nice somehow made it worse. I was just about to head over to your house and bring you this to say sorry."

At that, Fergus felt himself brim with relief. "So . . . " he tried. "Fancy watching the race? If Mrs D doesn't mind me staying, that is. I've brought crisps too!" And he held up a packet of cheese and onion – Daisy's favourite.

Daisy shook her head. "Mum won't let me eat on the sofa," she said.

"Oh," said Fergus, remembering. "It was just an idea." And he turned to go.

"Well, I've got a better one," said Daisy.

Fergus swung back round.

"How about we go back to yours and get Sorcha over and we can all watch it together? Plus, I bet she has better taste in bridesmaids' dresses than your mum. Maybe she can help make sure I'm not dressed like a lampshade?"

Fergus laughed. "Well, she certainly couldn't make it worse! Brilliotic!"

That afternoon, as the three friends sat cross-legged on the sofa eating marmalade sandwiches, watching Spokes cycle to his fiftieth historic victory, Fergus felt he'd never been happier. He just hoped Daisy was as happy too.

"See how he slid out of that slipstream?" Daisy said. "That's what you've got to do, Fergus. I've been watching you, and I really think you're coming out too quick. Just hold on for that extra second and it'll make all the difference."

Fergus nudged her. "You know I can't do this without you," he said.

She nudged him back. "I know," she said.

"How about these?" asked Mum, holding up a picture of a bright violet bow tie and bridesmaid's sash.

Daisy shrugged worriedly. But Sorcha grabbed her pad and wrote in massive capital letters:

> *TOO PURPLE!*

Daisy and Fergus grinned.

"Okay, okay, back to the drawing board," said Mum, picking up the magazine and flicking again.

Fergus took the pad and pen. "And we couldn't do this without you," he wrote back. "Thanks, Sorcha."

"Friends first and forever," Daisy added in her own looped handwriting. And then, one by one, they signed it.

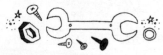

"Fits nicely, doesn't it," said Grandpa, coming to say goodnight and noticing the note Fergus had pinned up in the space where the Spokes poster had once taken pride of place.

"It's perfect," said Fergus. "Everything's perfect."

And even if perfect only lasted another few weeks, it was worth it for the way he felt now: like nothing could touch him. He had a place on the team, he had a fabulous family, and best of all, he had his friends. First and forever.

And that was better than any medal.

And we couldn't do this without you. Thanks, Sorcha

Friends first and forever

Fergus

Sorcha

Daisy

Joanna Nadin is an award-winning author of more than seventy books for children, including the bestselling Rachel Riley diaries, the Penny Dreadful series, and *Joe All Alone*, which is now being adapted for TV. She studied drama and politics at university in Hull and London, and has worked as a lifeguard, a newsreader and even a special adviser to the Prime Minister. She now teaches writing and lives in Bath, where she rides her rickety bicycle, but she never, ever back-pedals...

www.joannanadin.com

Clare Elsom is an illustrator of lots of lovely children's books, including the Furry Friends series, the Spies in Disguise series, the Maisie Mae series, and many more. She studied Illustration at Falmouth University (lots of drawing) and Children's Literature at Roehampton University (lots of writing). Clare lives in Devon, where she can be found doodling, tap dancing and drinking cinnamon lattes.

www.elsomillustration.co.uk